How Do Yo

She seemed to hear Kate's voice saying, "There's nobody like Annie. Nobody!"

TOUCHED
BY AN
ANGEL

How Do You Spell Faith?

Novelization by Monica Hall
Based on a teleplay by
Michael Glassberg

Martha Williamson
Executive Producer

Based on the television
series created by
John Masius

Tommy
NELSON
Thomas Nelson, Inc.
Nashville

How Do You Spell Faith?
Book Three in the *Touched By An Angel* fiction series.

Touched By An Angel is a trademark of CBS Broadcasting Inc. Used under license.

Copyright © 1999 CBS Worldwide, Inc.

How Do You Spell Faith? novelization by Monica Hall is based on a teleplay by Michael Glassberg.

Published in Nashville, Tennessee, by Tommy Nelson™, a division of Thomas Nelson, Inc. Vice President, Children's Books: Laura Minchew; Managing Editor: Beverly Phillips.

Library of Congress Cataloging-in-Publication Data

Hall, Monica.
How do you spell faith? / novelization by Monica Hall.
p. cm.—(Touched by an angel)
"Based on a teleplay by Michael Glassberg; Martha Williamson, executive producer; based on the television series created by John Masius."
Summary: While preparing for a spelling bee with the help of an angel disguised as a tutor, thirteen-year-old Annie is discouraged that her mother keeps comparing her with her more athletic older sister.
ISBN 0-8499-5804-0
[1. Mothers and daughters—Fiction. 2. Sisters—Fiction. 3. Death—Fiction. 4. English language—Spelling—Fiction. 5. Guardian angels—Fiction. 6. Angels—Fiction.] I. Glassberg, Michael. II. Touched by an angel (Television program) III. Title. IV. Series.
PZ7.H14725Ho 1999
[Fic]—DC21

98–51077
CIP
AC

Printed in the United States of America
99 00 01 02 03 QPV 9 8 7 6 5 4 3 2 1

Contents

Contents

The Characters

Annie Gibson, a bright, solitary thirteen-year-old with a very special gift, who learns that 'love' and 'faith' are more than just words in a dictionary.

Kate Gibson, Annie's beloved big sister, a star athlete and local hero. She is the light of Annie's life. Annie feels Kate and their father are the only people who really appreciate her talent.

Mary Gibson, Annie and Kate's athletic mother, who bonded easily with her athletic daughter Kate, but still struggles to understand her younger daughter.

Sondra Adams, the brisk, busy school principal, who forgets that there is more than one way to define 'success'—until an angel reminds her.

Coach Liz Higby, the high school basketball coach whose women's team—led by Kate—is on the verge of winning the division finals.

The Characters

Tess, a wise, supervising angel with a warm heart and a no-nonsense attitude. She is sent by God to help Mrs. Gibson understand that there's more than one way to spell 'love'. She appears this time as a substitute teacher.

Monica, a joyful angel, who delights in each new assignment and turns out to know more about spelling than she thought she did. She is sent by God to help and encourage Annie. She appears this time as a spelling tutor.

Andrew, a strong, compassionate angel, whose job is to help people find their way home—whether that means heaven or their home on earth. He appears this time as a taxi-cab driver.

Introduction

The banner above the trophy case billowed every time the doors to Olympus High opened. It almost seemed to shout its message to the busy hallway.

SEMIFINALS FRIDAY! GO LADY TITANS!

The students rushing by agreed completely. Olympus High had a championship basketball team, and they wore its colors with pride. In green and silver jackets, sweaters, backpacks, and caps, the noisy crowd scrambled through the last precious minutes before first bell. But no one noticed the two observers standing by locker 127, smiling at the early morning chaos.

As she watched, Monica could barely contain herself. "I just love school, Tess! An entire building completely devoted to learning. And I'm all prepared," she assured her supervisor, rummaging through her green and silver book bag. "I bought new pens and pencils, a spiral notebook—"

Tess peered into the bag. "Anything in there for me?"

Monica grinned and pulled out a shiny red apple.

Tess nodded. "You've just earned your first A, Miss Wings."

"A is for *Apple*," Monica recited playfully. Then she raised a questioning eyebrow. "Or maybe A is for *Assignment*?"

Tess nodded. "How's your spelling, Angel Girl?"

"Well . . . okay, I guess. Are there many long words?"

"Oh, yes," said Tess. "Long words. Short words. All kinds of words. And *some* of them say a lot *more* than some people hear."

Monica looked worried. "Never mind, baby," said Tess. "You'll know what you need to know when the time comes. Just count on God, and have—"

"Faith," Monica finished and smiled. "And that's a word I *do* know how to spell!"

Chapter One

Out of Step

Monica eagerly searched the crowded hallway. "Which one is she, Tess?"

Tess pointed to the only student *not* moving at warp speed. "She's over there, baby."

A slight figure with her brown hair pulled back in a ponytail, drifted slowly down the hall, intently studying a pocket dictionary. She was a solitary little island in the rushing stream. An obstruction to traffic. A four-foot, nine-inch roadblock in the morning stampede, untouched by the commotion around her. When Annie Gibson had her nose in a dictionary, she forgot everything else as she quietly spelled the words to herself over and over.

Monica studied the thirteen-year-old. "Oh Tess, I feel so bad. I didn't even notice her."

Tess nodded. "That happens way too often around here." She winced as a group of boys accidentally bumped into Annie—girl, backpack, and book went flying. But Annie didn't miss a beat. She picked herself up, found her page, and went right on reading. "That little girl's even a mystery to her mother."

"Her mother?" Monica asked.

"Make that *especially* to her mother," said Tess. She nodded toward a slim woman in a delivery uniform hurrying down the hall. Quick and surefooted, Mary Gibson wove through the crowd with an athlete's ease and soon caught up with her daughter.

"You've got to start paying attention, Annie," she scolded, "or the whole world is going to knock you down! Even when it's, you know . . ."

"Inadvertent?" Annie offered. "I, N, A, D, V, E, R, T, E, N, T. Meaning 'unintentional'. From the middle Latin—"

Mrs. Gibson frowned. "If you keep this up, you'll *never* make any friends."

Annie's blue eyes finally focused on her mother. "What are you doing here, Mom?"

Mrs. Gibson held out a brown bag. "You left your lunch in the car, *again*."

"Oh, thanks." Annie tucked the bag in her backpack, turned a page, and headed down the hall.

"Don't forget to stop by the grocery store

after school," her mother reminded her. "Harry has the list. All you have to do is pick up the order."

Annie nodded absently.

"Right after school, Annie!" her mother called. "No excuses."

With her nose back in her book, Annie nodded again. Mrs. Gibson shook her head, then hurried off to work.

Monica looked on the bright side. "Well, she may have a wee problem with her mother. But she certainly doesn't have a problem with words."

"That girl loves words," Tess agreed. "She studies them. She *spells* them. She *memorizes* them. Annie loves words the way some kids love sports, or clothes, or pizza!"

Monica was puzzled. "Well, that's good, isn't it?"

"It's her gift . . . and her handicap," Tess explained. "You see, baby, words can be used to express wonderful thoughts and ideas. But they can also be used to hide from the world."

"Is that Annie's problem?" asked Monica.

Tess nodded. "Annie only feels truly connected to three things in her life: words, her father, and . . ." Tess pointed to a group of seniors.

Monica knew instantly which one Tess meant—the tall, slender girl with the dancing braid of hair that swished behind her. She was all joy and quicksilver energy, with a mouth made for laughter and eyes the same intense blue as Annie's. Even when perfectly still, she seemed to be in motion.

"That's Annie's sister, Kate," Tess said. "She's the star of the best women's basketball team this state has ever seen. A real local hero here in Olympus—and Annie's champion in life."

Just then Kate spotted her sister. She sped down the hall on graceful, silent feet and wrapped Annie in a surprise hug. "Hey, Little Sis, how's the family genius?"

A rare smile lit up Annie's somber little face.

Her book forgotten, she hugged her sister back.

Monica wanted to hug them both! "How wonderful to have a sister who cares so much. Not everyone is so blessed."

Tess slowly nodded. "That's true. But things are about to metamorphose, Angel Girl. And you've got to be there when it happens."

"Meta . . . what?"

Reaching into Monica's bag, Tess pulled out a dictionary.

"*Metamorphose*. Starts with an M. From the Greek: 'to transform'. Better study up, Miss Wings. A girl's future is at stake. And this time, spelling counts!"

Chapter Two

Define Success

As the last classroom door banged shut, Tess stood perfectly still, just enjoying the quiet. Then with her sign-up sheet in hand, she stepped up to the big bulletin board.

With a friendly nod to Principal Sondra Adams, she looked for a place to post her notice. But every inch was filled—mostly with basketball schedules, clippings, and posters. *Not a smidgen of space is left for something academically important,* thought Tess. *Well, we'll see about that!*

Principal Adams looked at the full bulletin board with pride. "This is an exciting time for us, Tess."

Tess raised one eyebrow. "All this fuss over a little basketball game?"

"There's nothing little about it," Principal Adams answered sharply.

Tess eyed the brisk, silver-haired woman thoughtfully. *Hmm, a lady with strong opinions. I can understand that. I've been known to express an opinion or two of my own from time to time.*

"Kate Gibson has put this town on the map again," the principal continued. "Do you know how many college recruiters are after that girl?"

Tess nodded. "That's good," she agreed, then added, ". . . for Kate Gibson."

"That's good for all of us," Principal Adams corrected firmly. "It makes the whole school look good. It makes the whole school feel good. Success breeds success!" She glanced at her watch. "I'll check in with you after class."

Tess studied the packed bulletin board a moment longer. Then, with a firm punch of a tack, she posted her sign-up sheet smack-dab in the middle of the biggest GO LADY TITANS poster!

It was barely in place when she had her first 'customer'.

Annie Gibson—late for class as usual—read the notice with interest. Then she fished a pen out of her backpack and signed her name.

"Well, congratulations, Annie Gibson!" Tess beamed. "You're the first to sign up."

Annie shrugged. "And probably the last. Nobody ever signs up to take the qualifying test for the Midwest Regional Spelling Bee."

"You just did," said Tess, with a satisfied smile.

"Well, you know, I'm . . ." Annie rolled her eyes at Tess, "'weird'. Spelling is the foundation of communication. But try telling that to the *illiterai* in this school!"

"Well, I think you have great potential," answered Tess. "You're such a good speller. You could easily win the spelling bee and bring home the title."

Annie grinned. "Potential. P, O, T, E, N, T, I, A, L. 'A latent excellence that may or may not be developed.'"

The principal's door whisked open. "Late again, Annie?" Principal Adams was frowning. "You should be in class."

She shook her head as Annie scooted away. "That girl!"

Tess pointed to the bulletin board. "She just signed up for the spelling bee."

Principal Adams sighed. "Well, I'm afraid she's going to be disappointed."

Tess stood a little taller. "Why?"

"We have limited funds for extracurricular programs, Tess. Do you know what it takes to send someone to a contest like that? We can't afford to fund it for just one student. And, believe me, no one else is interested."

"Because it's not basketball?" asked Tess.

Principal Adams nodded a resigned yes. "Kids today only care about things that can get them on a Wheaties box." Suddenly, that reason seemed a little lame. "It's a different time from when we were young, Tess."

"And success breeds success?"

"Exactly," agreed the principal, relieved.

"Then . . ." began Tess thoughtfully, "if one kid succeeds at the spelling bee this year, others will try next year and—"

"We can't afford it, Tess," Principal Adams said quickly. "There would have to be a chaperone . . . a tutor . . . someone—"

"I know someone who'd just love to volunteer," Tess quickly offered.

Principal Adams made one last try. "A qualified semantics coach?"

Tess's eyes lit up. "Qualified beyond your wildest dreams," she promised.

Chapter Three

D Is for *Differences*

Kate Gibson's trademark braid whipped in an arc as she swerved left. The heavy woven strands flicked under the nose of the startled guard, and with a laughing glance at her opponent, Kate changed direction again. Her path was clear! Her long legs flashing, she drove the ball down the court.

"GO, KATE," called Annie, in a very un-Annie-like shout. She held her breath as her sister sprang into the air. Up flew Kate. Higher and higher. She hovered a long moment in a slant of late afternoon sunlight. Then her slender body curved forward as she reached out with the ball and sank the basket!

"YES!" Annie jumped to her feet, prized dictionary flying. "Yes!" There was nobody like her sister. Nobody!

Kate looked across the floor, caught her little sister's eye, and winked.

Annie grinned back, then sank to her seat in the noisy gym. It was only a practice, but the bleachers were filled with students cheering. Game or workout, watching their team—

and Kate—was always exciting. How could they not sweep the division finals? Their team was a wonder! And Kate was its heart.

"Excuse me," said a soft voice. "Are you Annie Gibson?"

Annie jumped. She wasn't used to being noticed.

"Yes," Annie said as she studied the young woman in the green and silver sweatshirt.

"My name is Monica. I'm a spelling tutor. And I'd like very much to help you get ready for the qualifying test on Friday."

Annie frowned. "I'm already ready! Who says I need help?"

Monica smiled. "Someone who thought that my loquaciousness might be an asset."

"Loquaciousness?" Annie repeated. That was a new one!

"L . . . O . . . Q . . . ?"

Monica helped finish. "U, A, C, I, O, U, S, N, E, S, S."

Very impressed, Annie opened her dictionary and looked up the word. She read: "Talking or tending to talk much or freely.

Loquaciousness." Looking up at Monica she said, "Good one."

"Well," said Monica modestly, "if you're going to be a spelling tutor you need to be able to spell. I didn't mean to cast aspersions on your ability, Annie. I'm sure you're already doing very well. I'm only here to help if you want my help."

Annie thought it over. "Well . . . I guess it would be fun to have somebody to train with. Kinda like Kate does."

Monica's eyes followed Annie's. "Is that your sister?"

Annie beamed. "Yeah. She's the greatest!" Then she looked at her watch. "Oh, no!" She snapped her dictionary shut, grabbed her jacket and backpack . . . and bolted. "I gotta go!"

Mrs. Gibson frowned at her mismatched living room furniture. She really should get slip-covers—or something. Maybe one of these days. Then she grinned. Who was she kidding? Style just wasn't her strong point. Oh well, at least they had a roof over their heads. And a clean place to live. In fact, the Gibson trophy collection positively gleamed!

Gently, she touched the eager runner atop the biggest trophy of all. Mrs. Gibson's mouth turned up in a smile as she remembered the day she won it.

For a moment, Mrs. Gibson was eighteen again. Heart pounding, feet skimming the cinder track, she ran . . . she flew! State champion! But it wasn't just the winning that she missed. It was the *doing*. And, oh, she'd done it well!

If only I'd been able to take that college scholarship, she thought. *If only . . .*

Her eyes snapped open. *Never mind! We're doing fine, just fine.* With a farewell pat for the trophy's small runner, she straightened Kate's basketball awards. *The Gibson family* still *has a star athlete. And it's all just beginning for Kate.*

The doorbell interrupted her thoughts.

D Is for *Differences*

When she opened the front door Harry Peterson's friendly grin was beaming over the top of two big grocery bags. "Figured when Kate's little sister didn't come by, I'd better bring this over myself. Wouldn't want to disrupt Kate's training schedule."

"Thanks, Harry." Mrs. Gibson sighed. She took the bags as they began to slip from his arms.

"So, Friday's the big day, huh?" he asked.

Mrs. Gibson nodded. "Last game before division finals."

"Bound to win," Harry predicted. "We've got a crackerjack team. And that Kate . . ." He gave an admiring whistle. "Best athlete this town's had since . . . I guess, since *you*."

She smiled and shook her head. "Thanks, but that was a long time ago. My sprinting days are over."

Harry bounced on his toes. "Well, Kate's been a real godsend these past couple of years. Finally, this town's got something to be excited about again."

"Yes, I'm very proud of her." Mrs. Gibson

looked into the bag, surprised. "Harry, I didn't order some of this stuff."

Harry waved a big hand. "Just threw in a few things for Kate. Like those yogurt-covered nuts she likes. They're on the house."

"Thanks, Harry." She smiled. "That's very sweet."

"Oooof . . ." Harry answered, as Annie charged through the door and right into him.

"Oh, sorry," she apologized.

"S'okay, kid." Harry shook his head as he left. *I never can remember that girl's name. Little bit of a thing. Not at all like her sister, Kate. Not at all.*

Mrs. Gibson glared at Annie. "See what happens when you don't pay attention? Harry came all the way over here, out of his way, because you forgot, *again*. And don't give me that line about migitat . . ."

"Mitigating circumstances," said Annie helpfully. "M, I, T, I—"

"Stop it, Annie," Mrs. Gibson snapped. "Don't correct your mother. Nobody talks that way."

"Monica does," said Annie, eager to share her news. "She's going to help—"

Mrs. Gibson wasn't listening. "Why don't you get out a little and get some exercise? You spend too much time just sitting around spelling everything."

Annie's excitement drained away. "I'm not like you and Kate, Mom," she said quietly. "I'm xenogenic."

"You're what?" Mrs. Gibson's voice slid up the scale.

"Xenogenic," Annie repeated. "X, E, N, O, G, E, N, I, C. Xenogenic. From the Greek *xenos* meaning 'foreigners' and *genic* meaning 'from the genes'—completely and permanently different from the parent."

Mrs. Gibson just stared at her daughter. What could she say? It was true. She often felt that this clever, and sometimes irritating, child of hers might as well be from another planet!

Chapter Four

Connections

The night wind slipped through the cracks in the old tree house. It peeked under the papers on the battered table, played with a pile of leaves in the corner, then rattled the big world map on the wall—knocking two of the colored pins loose. One in Brazil. One in Russia.

The figure seated at the shortwave radio didn't notice. Ink-stained fingers carefully adjusted a dial. "CQ, CQ, CQ, 20 meters to U, N, three, R, H. This is K, zero, XBX," said a soft voice. "CQ, CQ, CQ, 20 meters to UN3RH, this is K, zero, XBX. You out there?"

With a crackle of static, a booming Russian voice replied, "Reading you, K, zero, XBX. This is UN3RH."

"Hey, Boris."

Halfway around the world, Boris chuckled. "Hello, Kate Gibson. How is the famous American basketball star? Ready for the championship game?"

"Indubitably," came the reply, "I, N, D . . ." *Whoops!* "I mean, yes. Hey, my little sister entered this spelling contest."

"She did? How do you think she'll do?"

"Great! But it's making our mom crazy."

"Knock, knock," called a playful voice.

Oh my gosh! "Sorry, gotta go, Boris. Have to
. . . have to go work out. K, zero, XBX, QRT—K,
zero, XBX clear." Annie Gibson twisted the dial
to OFF, just as Kate came into the tree house.

"Hey, Kate," said Annie. She studied her
big sister cautiously. *Had Kate heard?* She
couldn't tell, but she hoped not. She liked
pretending to be a star athlete with her shortwave friends—it didn't hurt anyone.

Kate drifted over to the big map. She gave an
approving nod at the dozens of bright-colored
pins dotting the world. Each one represented
one of Annie's shortwave pals. "My little sister
really gets around." Then she put a gentle hand
on Annie's shoulder. "You okay? I heard Mom
was pretty upset this afternoon."

Annie shrugged.

"Well, maybe this will cheer you up." Kate
reached inside her team jacket and pulled out
an envelope. "You got another one," she said,
handing it to her sister.

Annie beamed. "It's from Dad? Wow. That's already two this month!"

"He must be thinking about you a lot these days." Kate smiled as she watched her sister read the letter.

A troubled frown wiped the joy from Annie's face. "I wish Mom hadn't driven him away. Things would be a lot better around here."

"You can't blame Mom, sweetie. He walked out on us! Believe me, Annie, Dad was no picnic. Don't you remember the arguments? How much it bugged him the way Mom and I just wanted to do things instead of planning them out ahead of time?" For just a moment the strong, confident athlete looked like a lost little girl as she remembered their father.

Annie wasn't convinced. "Well, at least he doesn't think I'm a geek, like Mom does."

"Mom doesn't think you're a geek," Kate protested.

"Yes, she does." Her voice shook. "And she's right."

Connections

"Annie . . ." Kate's strong hands turned her little sister to face her. Blue eyes looked deep into blue eyes. "Don't you know how awesome you are?"

Annie blinked away tears. "All I can do is spell words."

Kate gave her a little shake. "All! I'd give a million dollars to spell like you do."

"Really?" Annie wanted to believe it.

"Believe it, Little Sis!" This was the Kate voice that never took 'no' for an answer. "God has a special gift for every person. Mom's and mine is for sports. Yours is for words. And your gift is going to take you a lot farther than mine ever will."

Annie felt ten feet tall. Strong. Invincible. Just like Kate. Then she remembered. "There's a qualifying test for the Midwest Regional Spelling Bee," she began, "but it's this Friday. Same time as your game." Annie had never missed one of Kate's games!

But Kate didn't see any problem. "Perfect," she announced. "I'll go to mine. You go to yours. And we'll both come home winners."

She winked, then picked up Annie's dictionary. Letting it fall open, she ran her finger down the page. Her eyes glinted playfully as she read out, "Mesembryanthemum."

Annie grinned. "From the Greek *mesembria* meaning 'midday,' and *anthemon* meaning 'flower'. M, E, S, E, M, B, R, Y, A, N, T, H, E, M, U, M. Mesembryanthemum."

Kate punched the air in a victory salute. "Yes!" she crowed. "She's amazing. She's a genius."

Annie giggled, then she threw her arms around Kate and hugged as hard as she could. *There's nobody like Kate. Nobody!* she thought.

Chapter
Five

High Hopes

The Friday afternoon sunlight sprinkled gold dust on the quiet girl at the window. The classroom was silent, except for faint 'oom-pahs' and drumbeats drifting in from outside.

"Well," said Tess softly, "I suppose we'd better get started. You ready?"

"I am," Monica answered, eyes troubled. "But I'm not sure Annie is."

Tess looked over at the small girl who loved big words. Her voice was tender. "That's why she's surrounded by angels, baby."

Monica joined Annie at the window. The parking lot was filled with cars and buses. It looked like not only the whole school, but the whole town, was going to the game!

They watched together as the last tuba was squeezed into the last bus. "Well," said Monica, "this is the big day."

"For Kate *and* for me," Annie answered. She was still looking for her sister. "They're not going to void the results because nobody else showed up, are they?" Kate was counting on her!

"No," Monica assured her, "the results will be valid. It's a written exam. You get an individual score just as if the room were filled. Are you ready?"

"There she is! In Coach Higby's car," said Annie. She watched as Kate's laughing face and slender arms poked up through the sunroof of the coach's car. She was holding a big green and silver sign high in the air:

VANQUISHER—MEANING WINNER! GO ANNIE!!!

Annie laughed and waved back at Kate. The two sisters grinned at each other as the coach's car led off the procession. But who was that man in the white suit in the backseat? Funny, he seemed to be looking right at Annie.

Monica caught her breath as she saw Andrew. Then she closed her eyes and said a silent prayer.

With a final wave for Kate, Annie turned from the window.

"I'm ready."

Monica smiled as she watched Annie brush a wandering strand of hair from her cheek. Another promptly drifted down to take its place. The last two hours had been an ongoing contest between Annie and her ponytail, which *insisted* on pulling loose from the scrunchie. No doubt about it, Annie's hair definitely had a mind of its own!

Annie finished writing out the ninety-ninth word and glanced at her watch. *Wow, that was a long test! But not really all that hard,* Annie thought. She looked up at Monica. *Just one more word to go.*

"Onomato . . . puh . . . poe?" Monica began.

Yes! "Onomatopoeia," finished Annie. "'The making of a word by imitation of a sound'. Like 'hiss' . . . or 'eeek'." She wrote it out with a flourish.

"Umm . . . yes," confirmed Monica. "Very good, Annie. We're finished. One hundred words. Now sign your name at the bottom."

Monica slid the test into an envelope and sealed it. "I'll deliver this myself, and we'll have the results in a couple of days. But I have a feeling you got them all right. Even that onomato . . . one."

"Then what happens?" asked Annie, tightening the scrunchie on her ponytail for the umpteenth time.

"Then," answered Monica, "you'll qualify to go to the Midwest Regional Spelling Bee Championship at the state capitol."

"Do they give a trophy?" Annie asked, trying to sound as if it didn't really matter.

"I believe they do . . ." Monica answered. Then she winked. "A big one."

Annie grinned. *Wouldn't it be great to have my own trophy in the Gibson Collection?* she thought.

With a soft knock, the classroom door swung open. It was Principal Adams and Tess. Monica looked quickly at Tess, who nodded sadly. But Annie was watching her principal.

Something was very wrong with Principal Adams. Annie had never seen her move so slowly or look so . . . so lost. "Principal Adams?"

The principal closed her eyes for a moment, then took a big breath. "Annie," the principal's voice was shaking, "your mother would like you to come home right now."

Annie was suddenly very scared. "What's the matter?"

Principal Adams tried to answer, but couldn't. A shiver ran up Annie's back. She couldn't seem to breathe.

Tess put a gentle hand on Annie's shoulder. "A truck . . ." she said, "a truck ran into Coach Higby's car on the highway about an hour ago. The coach is going to be fine. But Kate . . . baby, your sister did not survive."

Annie felt cold, cold as ice. She couldn't breathe. And Tess's voice seemed to be coming from very far away. "Kate? Kate is . . . is . . . ?" She couldn't say the word.

Tess put her arms around her. "Yes, honey," she said softly. "She is. She died instantly. She didn't feel any pain."

Annie just looked at her. She could hear the words, but they didn't make any sense. Nothing made sense. Nothing.

Chapter
Six

A Great Sadness

Hunched over the table in the tree house, Annie searched through her dictionary as she did everyday. *There! Another long, hard word I didn't know. That makes five. I've mastered them all. Just like every day. Today is just another day. Nothing special about it at all. If I just keep doing this everything will be okay,* Annie thought as she tried to ignore the knocking at the door.

"Annie?" called Coach Higby. "It's time to go."

"I told you, I'm not going," she answered.

Coach Higby tried again. "Don't you want to say . . . good-bye?"

"No! Go away!" she shouted. *There is no reason to say good-bye. Kate isn't dead . . . she isn't! It can't be true. I won't let it be true.*

Coach Higby looked down at Mrs. Gibson, who was standing very still in the small yard and staring straight ahead . . . at nothing.

"Leave Annie alone," she said, "if that's what she wants. She's a smart girl. She can decide on her own." Mrs. Gibson turned and walked away.

"Too smart for her own good, if you ask me," Coach muttered. "I don't understand you, Annie," she called, starting down the ladder. "How can you miss your own sister's funeral? It's just so . . . so wrong."

Annie leaned against the tree house wall. "Solecism," she recited softly. "A breach of good manners or etiquette." A single tear slid down her cheek and plopped onto the dictionary.

Every chair on the polished floor and every seat in the bleachers was full. The big gym was filled to the rafters. But this time there were no happy shouts and cheers. No pounding feet or thumping of a ball.

Every eye—every heart—was focused on the narrow box and mound of white flowers in center court. The entire town had come to say good-bye to its darling.

Still at home, Annie sat on the tree house floor with her back against the wall. She hadn't moved in a long time. And when someone knocked softly, she barely twitched. "Go away."

"Hello, Annie."

Monica? What is she doing here?

A long white envelope slid through a slit in the wall. "Congratulations. You qualified for the Midwest Regional Spelling Bee Champion-ship."

Annie barely glanced at the envelope. "So what?"

Monica's voice was tender. "Annie, I know this is a terribly painful time. But you've worked so hard. You have a right to be happy about this."

"Happy? Don't you get it? Kate's . . . dead. Dead!" Annie's voice shook. "Nothing matters. Especially a bunch of stupid words."

Monica leaned her head against the fragile wall that separated them. She had to get through to Annie. But how? Then she knew. Words! Of course.

"Did you ever think how important words are, Annie? If it weren't for words, where would we be? You can't build buildings without words. You can't govern a country or fly to the moon or even order dinner without words." She paused a moment. "And you can't say good-bye without words."

There was no answer. But Monica was not giving up. "Words are life, Annie. When you speak you give birth to your thoughts. You send them out into the universe, and suddenly they have power. Think about it. In the very beginning were God's words, Annie."

Monica's voice filled the small room. "Did you ever notice that God never did anything without putting it into words first? 'Let there be light,' He said, and there was light. He spoke the entire world into existence. And you can be sure He knew how to spell every word of it, too!"

She waited, but there was only silence. "God has given you a gift, Annie," she said firmly. "The gift of language and words—and the power that comes with them. He wants you to use that gift. Kate wants you to use it," she finished softly.

"Spelling isn't going to bring Kate back," answered Annie's cold, distant voice.

Chapter Seven

Saying Good-Bye

Annie waited until the last mourner had left. Then she slipped quietly into the empty gym. She stood as still as a stone just inside the doors, her eyes focused on the floor. Finally, she looked up. A last ray of afternoon sunlight haloed the mound of white flowers in center court. It glinted off a bronze handle and woke glimmers of red in the polished wood—wood the exact color of Kate's hair. *Kate! Oh, Kate. . . .*

Slowly, Annie stepped forward and rested her small hand on the casket. She didn't move for a long time. Finally, she reached into her pocket and took out her dictionary. She placed it gently on the lid, right over Kate's heart. Then she turned and walked away.

That evening the Gibsons' living room was filled with the clink of plates and glasses and the murmur of soft voices. Family and friends had gathered to offer what comfort they could.

Saying Good-Bye

Mrs. Gibson sat quietly on the sofa, trying very hard to pay attention to Principal Adams. But her thoughts kept wandering. So many memories . . .

"Kate was such a remarkable young woman," Principal Adams said. "The community has been trying to think of a way to honor her. How do you feel about a scholarship in Kate's name?"

"A scholarship?" Mrs. Gibson looked at Principal Adams for the first time. "To help another athlete?" She smiled. "Oh, yes. Yes . . . I think Kate would have liked that."

Principal Adams patted Mrs. Gibson's hand and stood up. "We'll take care of it."

Tess sat down next to Mrs. Gibson and held out a plate filled with food. Mrs. Gibson shook her head. With an understanding smile, Tess put the plate on a table. "There's a lot of food in that freezer, Mary," she said kindly. "Now you just be sure to eat some of it. It's not going to do you any good if you don't take care of yourself."

Mrs. Gibson nodded. "Thank you, Tess."

"How is Annie doing?" Tess asked.

Mrs. Gibson shrugged. "She's handling this the way she handles everything—all by herself." Her lips tightened. "Just like her father."

Tess knew all about that sad story. And she was sorry for it. But thinking about the past wasn't going to help this family now. "You know," she said brightly, "her tutor, Monica, says that Annie qualified for the Midwest Regional Spelling Bee Championship."

Mrs. Gibson wasn't interested. "Spelling Bee Championship?" *What did that matter?* she thought.

Tess's eyes were kind, but her voice was firm. "I know it's an awkward time, but your daughter had the highest score of all the contestants."

"Words," said Mrs. Gibson, shaking her head. She looked up as the front door opened. "Annie?"

But Annie didn't answer. She just kept walking.

"Annie!" Mrs. Gibson's voice was concerned, then angry, as Annie disappeared down the hallway. "Oh Tess, I just don't know how to get through to her."

The little tree house seemed especially empty that night. The dim light from the shortwave radio barely pushed back the shadows.

"I'm so sorry, Kate," said a voice with a soft Spanish accent. "Little Annie gone. I can't believe it."

Annie wiped away a tear. "Yeah," she said gruffly. "So, I've got to get going, Elena. And you're probably not going to hear from me for a while."

Her radio friend was surprised. "Where are you going?"

"As far from here as I can," Annie answered. "K, zero, XBX, QRT—K, zero, XBX clear."

Her hand shook as she stuffed the precious letters from her father into a big duffel bag filled with clothes. She smoothed Kate's team jacket with a gentle hand and zipped the bag shut.

Saying Good-Bye

With a final look around the little room, she reached out and turned the radio dial to OFF. It was her last connection to her old life.

Annie waited in the shadows until the 7:00 A.M. school bus chugged off down the street. Then she stepped up to the bus stop. But she didn't have to wait long. The Tri-State bus to Minneapolis was right on time.

Annie stumbled down the aisle as the bus whooshed away from the curb. If she'd looked out the window just then, she would have seen something very surprising. Standing there at the bus stop—the *deserted* bus stop she had just left—was the mysterious man in the white suit. The man who had been in the car with Kate and Coach Higby last Friday!

Chapter Eight

G Is for *Gone*

Annie dragged her duffel bag down the steps. The doors snapped shut behind her and, with a puff of exhaust, the Tri-State bus swept back into traffic.

Her blue eyes wide open, Annie stood stock-still in the middle of the busy sidewalk. She had no idea what to do next. There were so many people—all in a hurry. And Minneapolis was so . . . big. She looked at the envelope in her hand—the last letter she'd received from her dad. *How will I ever find that address?* she worried.

Tess and Monica smiled as Principal Adams posted the notice. For once, there was plenty of room on the big bulletin board. All the basketball posters and schedules were gone. The Kate Gibson Scholarship announcement stood alone.

"Wow," said a passing student, "I wonder what you have to do to win *that*?"

Principal Adams smiled sadly. "Well," she

assured him, "the winning candidate doesn't have to be *exactly* like Kate."

"Just championship material?" asked Tess innocently.

Principal Adams nodded, eyeing Tess cautiously. She remembered their last discussion at this board.

But it was Monica who spoke up. "I know someone who would be a *perfect* candidate for the Kate Gibson Scholarship. Someone who qualified for the Midwest Regional Spelling Bee Championship with the *highest* score. Annie Gibson."

Oh, dear, thought Principal Adams, *two of them?*

"Where *is* Annie?" asked Tess as the class bell rang.

Principal Adams was surprised. "Isn't she here?"

Monica shook her head. "No, she didn't show up today."

"That's odd," said Principal Adams with a frown. "Annie never misses school. She even tried to come when she had the mumps!"

"Well, I know her mother was going back to work today," said Tess.

Now Principal Adams looked downright worried. "I hope she's all right. Sometimes I think Kate was the only thing holding that child together."

Tess headed for the door. "This is my free period. Maybe I'll just check into this."

Mrs. Gibson backed the big delivery van up to the Global Parcel loading dock. *Time to get to work.* But she couldn't stop looking at Kate's picture on the dashboard.

"How are you doing, Mary?" It was Tess, waiting on the dock. Mrs. Gibson climbed down from the van. "Keeping busy," she answered abruptly as she opened the van's back doors. "Did you need something, Tess?"

Tess looked at her thoughtfully. "I wanted to talk to you about your other daughter."

Mrs. Gibson slid a carton off the dock into the van. "Annie's a smart kid. She'll be all right."

Tess nodded, handing Mrs. Gibson the next carton. "Yes, she's very smart. But brains don't have anything to do with the heart. And Annie's heart is just as broken as yours is right now."

Mrs. Gibson brushed away a tear with an impatient hand. "I know. But she doesn't share those things with me. She's got school, and I've got work. We'll get through it," she said as she picked up another carton.

"Annie didn't show up at school today." The words dropped like stones into the midday quiet. Mrs. Gibson spun around and stared at Tess.

Annie was tired. Her feet hurt. Her duffel bag seemed to have gained at least twenty pounds. And the best she could do was trudge along very slowly.

For the umpteenth time, she checked the address on the envelope. But none of the buildings on this street matched it either. What was she going to do?

"Need a taxi?" called a friendly voice.

Annie stared at the big yellow taxicab at the curb. Funny, the street had been empty a moment ago. Then she stared even harder at the smiling driver inside. Where had she seen him before?

"You look kind of familiar," she said.

He shrugged his big shoulders. "Could be," said Andrew, dressed in a denim shirt and jeans. "I get around."

That was no answer! She shook her head impatiently. What did it matter? He looked nice. It was a real taxi. And she couldn't walk another step!

"What does it cost?" she asked.

"How about ten dollars?" Andrew answered.

Annie was relieved. She had a little more than ten dollars in her pocket. Dragging her heavy duffel behind her, she climbed into the taxi.

The taxi moved slowly down another Minneapolis street. Annie stared anxiously out the window—as she had for the last thirty minutes.

"Do you want to just keep driving around?" Andrew asked pleasantly. "Or did you remember where you want to go?"

Annie jumped. "I don't know yet." She wished she didn't feel so nervous. "Do you have to keep asking me that?"

"Nope," came Andrew's cheerful response. "I could sing instead if you want. I do a great rendition of 'Danny Boy'."

That won a faint smile from Annie. "Rendition," she repeated absently, still staring out the window. "R, E, N, D, I, T, I, O, N. From the Old French *rendre*, 'to give back'."

"Ah," approved Andrew, "a fellow connoisseur of linguistics."

Annie shrugged. "I used to be."

"Reinventing yourself, huh?"

"Yes," Annie agreed, straightening her drooping shoulders. "Yes! I'm starting over. That's why I'm going to see my dad. He'll appreciate whatever I do. He always does."

"Then Dad's it is," said Andrew. "What's the address?"

That question again! Annie thought. But she wasn't ready to admit defeat. She just needed a little more time. "Maybe . . . maybe I should get something to eat first."

Andrew was perfectly agreeable. "You're the boss."

Andrew's long arm reached across the seat with Annie's burger bag. "No pickles. Extra ketchup. Right?"

Annie inhaled. It smelled wonderful! "Thanks."

"So, it's been awhile since you've seen your dad, huh? You want a straw?" Andrew's voice was casual.

"Yes," answered Annie—to both questions. "I was just a kid when he left. But he writes me letters all the time. I have most of them in my bag." She fished in her duffel. "See?"

Andrew looked impressed. "That's a lot of letters. I guess somebody must care a lot about you."

Annie nodded. "Yes. He's proud of me. He understands. He's the only one left who does."

Andrew pretended not to notice the tears in her eyes. "What about your mother? Doesn't she understand you?"

"No," she said sadly. "Just my dad and my sister Kate do . . . did." Annie's voice shook as she corrected herself. "My mom only cared about Kate. And Kate . . . Kate died."

Andrew's voice was gentle. "It can be rough on a family when you lose somebody like that. But I'm sure your mom cares about you, too."

Annie shook her head. "It doesn't matter anymore." She bit into the burger.

Andrew started the engine. "You're off to start a new life, right?" He turned and reached out his hand. "By the way, my name's Andrew."

"Annie," she replied, shaking his hand

solemnly. "You could come with me and meet my dad," she offered. "If you want to."

Andrew smiled. "I'd love to come with you."

Chapter Nine

An Unwelcome Surprise

Andrew pulled the taxi to the curb and turned off the engine. Annie stared out the window in shock. "This can't be right!"

"This is the address, Annie," he assured her.

Annie's hand shook as she opened the door. She stood very still on the cracked sidewalk staring at a vacant lot! Andrew came around and stood beside her.

"I don't understand," she said. "How can this be where my father lives?"

"Your father doesn't live here, Annie," Andrew said gently.

"But in the letters he wrote . . . Why would he lie to me?" Annie's voice was filled with hurt. She ran to the taxi. Snatching the letters from her bag, she waved them under Andrew's nose. "See?" she said. "This is the address he puts on all the envelopes. Like last year when he sent me my dictionary. And I got this one right after my mom and I had a big fight." Annie paused. Something didn't seem quite right. "Wait a minute, how did he always know about those things?"

An Unwelcome Surprise

Andrew's face was kind, but he was giving her that 'look'. It was the same look she'd get from a teacher when she was missing something important. She looked at the envelopes again. This time—for the first time—she studied the postmarks.

"Brainard . . ." read Andrew over her shoulder. "Great Falls . . . Eau Claire . . ." Not one of the letters had come from Minneapolis!

But Annie wasn't ready to give up yet. "Those are all places where Kate played her away games." Her hopeful blue eyes met his serious brown eyes. "Dad must've been going to Kate's games!"

Andrew shook his head. "What if your dad wasn't going to Kate's games?"

Annie stared at him. "What do you mean?"

"Well . . . take a look at that handwriting," he said. "Is that your dad's writing, or does it look like—"

"Kate's . . ." Annie breathed. *Of course. Kate's. But why?*

Andrew helped her the last step of the way. "Maybe your sister loved you so much that she tried to give you something she thought you wanted," he said. "Maybe Kate wrote these letters and signed your father's name because . . ."

Annie stared at him stubbornly, not wanting to hear what he was saying! Her hand tightened into a fist, crushing the letters.

". . . because she loved you very much," Andrew went on. "Kate loved you, Annie. And no matter how busy she was, no matter how successful she was, she always had time for her little sister."

But there was no comfort for Annie in Andrew's words. "Kate wrote those letters?" Her small hand opened as she dropped the letters to the ground. "My father never cared about me either?"

"I know this is tough, Annie," said Andrew softly. "You've had a lot of loss in your life. And this is like losing your father all over again. I want you to know it's okay to be angry."

Angry? Angry didn't begin to describe it! she thought. "I'm not angry." Annie's voice was as cold as ice. "Everything is copacetic. C, O, P, A . . ."

Andrew put his hand gently on Annie's shoulder. He shook his head. "I think you are angry, Annie. And if you don't let it out, it'll eat you up inside. You've lost your sister. You've lost your father. Don't lose yourself, too."

Annie shrugged off his hand. *There isn't anything left to lose!* she thought. She turned and walked away. "Prevaricator. 'One who lies.' P, R, E, V . . ."

Andrew's heart went out to the lonely little figure heading off to who-knows-where. But he knew running away wasn't the answer. He caught up with her. "I know you're hurting, Annie. But, sooner or later, you're going to have to deal with these feelings."

Annie didn't seem to hear him. "Betrayal," she murmured to herself, still walking. "B, E, T, R, A . . ."

But Andrew refused to be ignored. He turned her to face him. "You need to go home, Annie. You and your mom can work things out. I know you can. Come on, get in the taxi. I'll take you."

Annie's eyes were empty, and her mind seemed a thousand miles away. Without another word she followed him back to the waiting taxi.

Chapter Ten

Discarded Dreams

The taxi stopped in front of the Gibson house. Andrew looked back at Annie. She'd been quiet as a mouse all the way back from Minneapolis. Not a word from the girl with all the words. "Annie, I know that if you'll reach out to your mother . . ."

"Inconsequential," came the answer. "I, N, C, O . . ."

Tess and the policeman watched Mary Gibson pace back and forth . . . back and forth . . .

Tess put out a gentle hand to stop her. "You're making me dizzy, baby."

Mrs. Gibson looked at her, startled. She'd forgotten anyone else was there. "It's what I do when I'm upset, Tess. I move. I run. I put on my track shoes and I run until I can't think anymore. I ran when Ed walked out on us. I ran after Kate died."

Tess put her arm around Mrs. Gibson's

stiff shoulders. "Well, baby, it's time to stop running."

Mrs. Gibson looked at her helplessly. "I don't know how."

Before Tess could answer, the front door swung open. Annie was home.

"Annie!" Mrs. Gibson ran to the door. She didn't know whether to hug or shake her silent daughter.

But Tess knew just what to say. "Welcome home, baby."

"Where have you been?" Mrs. Gibson demanded.

Annie looked at her mother. "I went to see Dad in Minneapolis," she answered in a flat little voice.

This was too much. "Of all the foolish things! What made you think he was in Minneapolis?"

"Empirical evidence," answered the old Annie. "E, M, P, I—"

"Stop it," snapped her mother. "Just stop it, Annie!"

For once, that angry voice didn't make

Annie feel bad. She didn't feel much of any-thing. "The letters," she answered coldly.

"The letters?" Mrs. Gibson had no idea what Annie was talking about.

But Tess did. She picked up an envelope from the hall table. "You mean, like this one?"

"Let me see that," said Mrs. Gibson, reach-ing for the letter.

But Annie snatched it away. "It's mine! It's addressed to me."

Mrs. Gibson didn't understand any of this. "Who is it from?"

Annie studied the Minneapolis return address—and the postmark. "Kate. Kate wrote them. She wrote them all. She signed them from Dad and she sent them to me."

"But why?" asked her mother.

The icy little shell around Annie began to crack. "Because . . ." Her voice shook. "Because you don't believe in me."

Mrs. Gibson was stunned. "I believe in you," she protested.

"No, you don't. You believed in Kate." Annie shook her head.

"A lot of people believe in you, Annie," Tess said gently.

"In fact, they've decided to give the Kate Gibson Scholarship money to you—to pay your way to the Midwest Regional Spelling Bee Championship at the state capitol."

But it was way too late for that! Suddenly, quiet little Annie was furious. "I'm not going to the stupid spelling bee!" she shouted, running from the room.

Mrs. Gibson started to take a step after Annie, but instead sank slowly down onto the sofa. Tess shook her head sadly. "That's not the same little girl that used to take such joy in words. We're losing her, Mary."

"I don't know what to say to her, Tess. I never know what to say." Tears filled Mrs. Gibson's eyes. "I know parents aren't supposed to have favorites. But, God help me, Kate was mine!"

Tess knew better. "No, she wasn't. You just

connected with Kate because she was like you."

Mrs. Gibson shook her head. "It's more than that. You want to know the real truth? Every time I look at Annie I see my ex-husband, Ed. Annie looks just like him. She acts like him. She even dreams like him. Ed always had his nose in a book, too."

Mrs. Gibson fell silent, remembering old hurts. Then she looked up. "Maybe I wasn't smart enough for Ed. And what . . . what if I'm not smart enough for my daughter?" Her tears overflowed, and she buried her face in her hands.

This was awful. She never cried! Embarrassed, she looked up at Tess—a very different Tess. She was . . . she was glowing! "What's going on here?" Mrs. Gibson quavered.

"I'm an angel, Mary," Tess said calmly. "Sent by God to bring you one simple word: 'truth'."

Mrs. Gibson inched back into the corner of the sofa. "An angel? Oh God, I've completely lost my mind."

Tess smiled. "No, baby. You've just lost your way. And God wants to help you get back on track."

Mrs. Gibson shook her head. "Annie and I are just different, Tess. Like Ed and I were. They're students. Kate and I were athletes. I don't know how to get through to somebody like that. I never did."

"Well, for starters," Tess said firmly, "you can stop looking at the differences and start trying to find some common ground." Her voice grew softer. "And you'd better do it quickly. Because if you keep running, Mary, you're going to run right past your daughter."

But Mrs. Gibson had no idea how to even begin. "I'm . . . I'm just not . . . good with words, Tess . . . not like Annie. The ones I need are never . . . there!"

Tess shook her head. "This isn't about who's smarter than who or who knows the most words. It's about a little girl who needs her mother. And you're the only one she's got. You know what else? She's all *you've* got."

Tess took Mrs. Gibson's hand. "Now,

whether you know it or not, God loves you. And that little girl loves you. She may not say it. But she spells it out for you every day. That's L, O, V, E, baby. Love."

Love? The word washed over Mrs. Gibson like sunshine in a dark room. *All those times Annie had tried to share her gift. All the ways she tried to make me proud. Love! How could I have missed what those long words were really saying?!* She looked at Tess with hopeful eyes. Maybe it wasn't too late.

Chapter Eleven

Plain Speaking

Mrs. Gibson looked up at the dark tree house. She took a big breath and planted her feet firmly—like a racer in the starting blocks. "Annie? Can you hear me?"

Silence was her only answer. "Well, I know you can, so I'm just gonna go ahead and say what I'm gonna say," she called. "I'm sorry, Annie. I . . . I guess I haven't been a very good mother. But I didn't mean to make you think you weren't important."

Oh, this was harder than any race she'd ever run! "I'm not very good with words, Annie. Not like you. You can do something I can't and that . . . that scared me. I thought you wouldn't love me, that you wouldn't respect me. But . . . I guess . . . maybe it's okay for kids to know something their parents don't. Maybe we can learn from each other."

She waited a moment for an answer that didn't come. "Anyway, I know you're pretty upset with me right now. And I don't blame you. I just want you to know that I love you. And I'm very proud of you."

Mrs. Gibson stood beneath the tree house for a long time. Then she walked slowly back to the house.

Inside the tree house, Annie worked very hard at not listening. But her mother's words kept repeating themselves in her head. Over . . . and over again. *Well, it's too late!*

She blinked as the radio dial suddenly lit up. "Hi, Annie. It's Andrew." She stared at the glowing dial. She hadn't turned the radio on! "Andrew," the voice repeated, "your friendly taxicab driver. Annie?"

She must be imagining things! "I know you're there, Annie," Andrew insisted. "And I have a message for you."

This is crazy! Annie crawled under the table and pulled the plug. She peeked cautiously at the radio. Good! The dial was dark. *Just my imagination,* she thought, picking up Kate's last letter—still unopened.

The radio lit up again. "Don't be afraid,

Annie. But this message is going to come through one way or the other. Know why? 'Cause God is sending it."

Now her eyes were as big as saucers. Annie fumbled with the dial. "K, zero, XBX, clear," she whispered. *Time to go in the house!* She jumped up . . . and ran right into Andrew!

"Do you believe in angels?" he asked as if they were just continuing a conversation.

"Celestial . . ." Annie's voice shook. "C, E, L, E . . ."

Andrew smiled and shook his head. "There is a time for everything, Annie. A time to live. A time to die." His smile grew a little bigger. "A time to spell. And a time to stop spelling . . . or doing anything that gets in the way of feeling what you need to feel."

Annie was all out of words. She just stared at Andrew.

And when he started to . . . to glow, it hardly made any difference. She was already as amazed as one small girl could possibly be. Then, all at once, she knew why he had seemed so familiar in Minneapolis. "In the car with Kate. In the backseat. That was you!"

Andrew nodded. "Yes. I was with your sister when she died."

"Take me to her," Annie begged.

Andrew shook his head. "I can't do that. I'm here to help you live."

That was too much! Angel or not, she was furious with him. "You didn't help Kate!"

Andrew understood. "I did help her, Annie. I helped her get to where she needed to go. And I'm here to help you do the same. Just as Kate fulfilled a wonderful purpose in her life by using the talent God gave her, so can you."

Annie turned away.

Andrew's voice was gentle. "Did you read the last letter Kate sent you?"

"Deception," Annie said coldly. "D, E, C, E, P, T, I, O, N!" She angrily tore the envelope to shreds and threw the pieces on the floor.

Andrew bent down and gathered the pieces. "No," he said, "it's the truth. These are the words Kate wanted to share with you."

And when he handed Annie the envelope it was as good as new!

Annie's glare refused both envelope and Andrew. So he opened it for her and began to read Kate's words:

Hey, Annie.
Just wanted to drop you a quick note to tell you to knock 'em dead at the spelling bee. I know you'll do it. You're the smartest kid I know. But you know what? Winning a spelling bee just means you're a good speller. Like winning a basketball game only means you can play basketball. You're more than that, Annie. You're a great kid. And I'm proud of you. Really proud. I wish I could be there to see it. . . .

"Abandoned," said Annie. "A, B, A, N, D, O, N, E, D."

Andrew studied her stubborn face. "I know why you like words so much," he said. "They're dependable. They don't go away. They're not going to leave you when things get bad." His voice was tender. "They're not going to die and leave you alone."

"Forsaken," said Annie. "F, O, R, S, A, K, E, N."

But Andrew wasn't giving up. "Words can build bridges or words can build walls. God wants you to use your words to build a bridge, Annie. To truth . . . to healing . . . and to your mother."

"Isolation," Annie answered. "I, S, O, L, A, T, I, O, N."

Andrew took her hands in his. "You are never isolated from God, Annie. He will never leave or forsake you. That's the difference between people and God. No matter how hard they try, people sometimes let you down. God never will," he said firmly. "Because God loves you perfectly."

Annie was silent.

"Unconditionally," Andrew said. "U, N, C, O, N, D, I, T, I, O, N, A, L, L, Y." Still no response. "Irrevocably," he tried. "'Incapable of being taken away.'" His eyes gleamed. "Unrefutably. U, N, R—"

"That's not a word!" said Annie, indignant.

Andrew grinned. "I know." Then he grew very serious. "Annie, God does love you! You are His beautiful child. Let Him be your father . . . your friend . . . now. Trust Him with the things that frighten you and the things that hurt you. Trust Him with your hopes and your dreams. He wants to be the best friend you've ever had."

Annie's mouth trembled. "God likes me?" she asked, afraid to believe, but wanting to believe what Andrew said.

Andrew swept away her last doubt. "A lot! He thinks you're great. And He's so sorry that you hurt so much."

Annie's tears overflowed. But an angel's shoulder, as it turns out, is perfectly water-proof. And very comforting.

Chapter Twelve

An Important Message

Mrs. Gibson ran a gentle finger over the framed photo. Arms around each other, Kate and Annie grinned back at her. She'd never understood the powerful connection between the two of them. *But maybe you don't have to understand love,* she thought. *Maybe you just have to let it be what it is.*

"Mom?" said a small voice from the hall.

For a long moment Annie and her mother just looked at each other. Then—though neither one remembered moving—they were holding each other tight. And it was very hard to tell whose tears were whose.

"I'm so sorry, Annie."

"Me, too, Mom."

Mrs. Gibson smoothed Annie's wayward hair. "I really am proud of you, sweetheart."

"Even if I'm never going to be any good at sports?" Annie asked.

That won a shaky smile. "Well," Mrs. Gibson said, "I'm probably not ever going to be a champion speller. But I love you, honey. With all my heart."

Annie snuggled closer. "I love you, too, Mom."

It sounded as if Monica said, "The word is 'gang'."

"Easy," answered Annie. "G, A, N, G. Gang."

"Wrong," said Monica. She smiled at Annie's surprised face. "Always ask the pronouncer for a definition, Annie. Remember? This *gangue* is French, from the Greek."

"Oh . . ." said Annie, a light dawning. "So, it's G, A, N, G, U, E."

"Exactly right," said Monica, her point made. "Do you want to try another?"

Annie nodded. "You're going to come with me and Mom to the finals, right?"

Monica shook her head. "I'm afraid not, Annie. God has something else for me to do that day. But a very good friend of mine has asked to go in my place."

God? wondered Annie, confused. Then her face lit up as Andrew walked into the room.

She smiled shyly at him, her mind racing. *Monica's friend? Does that mean she's an angel, too?*

But Monica just smiled and hugged her. "I'll be waiting right here at the school when you get back. I'm so proud of you."

Annie's smile got even bigger. She still wasn't used to hearing those words. But she liked them just fine.

Waiting nervously for the spelling bee to start, Annie tucked a lock of hair back behind her ear. Then she smoothed the skirt of her new blue outfit. It was the exact color of her eyes, her mom said when they had picked it out.

Annie wished they'd start! She stole another quick look around the auditorium. Everything was so big. And so many people filing in! Especially over . . . there.

Annie's mouth dropped open as she watched row after row fill up with green and silver. Hats. Jackets. Sweatshirts! Her school and town had come to cheer on one of their own.

When two of Kate's teammates jumped up with a big GO ANNIE! sign, she thought her heart would stop. And for just a moment—although she knew it was impossible—she seemed to hear Kate's voice saying, *"There's nobody like Annie. Nobody!"*

"Now take your time, Annie," said the pronouncer kindly. "The word is 'Kazakhstan'."

Yes! Annie smiled. "Kazakhstan," she repeated. "K, A, Z, A, K, H, S, T, A, N. Kazakhstan."

"That is correct," he confirmed.

"Yes!" cheered the crowd—especially the green and silver section. Tess waved her pennant. And at the side of the stage, Mrs. Gibson and Andrew traded jubilant high-fives.

It had been a long afternoon, filled with very long words. One by one, the other spellers had been eliminated. Now it was down to just two—Annie and Lori, the tall blond girl waiting for the next word.

"One of you will be the next Midwest Regional Champion," said the pronouncer. "All right, Lori, are you ready?" Lori nodded.

"The word is 'saponaceous'."

Uh-oh, thought Annie.

Lori took a long, big breath and began. "Saponaceous. S . . . A, P . . . O, N, A, C . . ." She hesitated, then finished in a rush, "I, O, U, S. Saponaceous."

Everyone waited. "I'm sorry," said the pronouncer. "That is incorrect."

Lori blinked back tears and walked to her chair. Annie knew just how she felt. Now it was her turn.

"Annie," said the pronouncer, "if you get this word correct and can spell the next word . . . you will be the new champion."

I know . . . I know! Annie thought as she closed her eyes.

The pronouncer's voice seemed to come from very far away. "The word is 'saponaceous'."

"From the Latin?" Annie asked, her voice almost steady.

He nodded yes.

"Saponaceous," she began. "S, A, P, O, N, A, C . . . E, O, U, S. Saponaceous."

No one breathed. Finally—after what felt like a year or two—the pronouncer nodded. "That is correct. One more and you will be the winner. Are you ready, Annie?"

Ready? She could barely move her head to nod.

"For the championship," he continued, "the word is 'rapprochement'."

Time seemed to stop. *Why couldn't it be a word I'm absolutely sure of?* Annie didn't know what to do. Then she remembered what Monica had said. "May I have the definition, please?"

"From the French," said the pronouncer. "The state of reconciliation. To make friendly again after an estrangement."

Oh, it was the perfect word after all— whether she could spell it or not! Annie looked over at her mother and smiled.

Mrs. Gibson smiled back and held up her own sign: "I Love You. L, O, V, E!"

Her eyes glowing with tears, Annie began. "Rapprochement. R, A, P, P, R . . ." Then she hesitated . . .

Back in Olympus, Monica was standing at the classroom window. Waiting. Her slender fingers tapped on the open dictionary. Angels are, of course, models of patience. But sometimes . . .

The classroom door flew open, followed by a blue-eyed whirlwind. "I remembered what you said," Annie bubbled. "I remembered to ask for the definition. But, then, I was so nervous I couldn't remember if it was 'O, A, C, H, E' or just 'O, C, H, E' . . ."

"So what did you do?" Monica asked.

"This time, I asked God to help me make the right decisions in my life—whether I won or lost the spelling bee," said Annie.

"And . . . ?" prompted Monica.

"And . . ." said Annie, sweeping a hand toward the door as Tess and Andrew came through it carrying an *enormous* trophy.

"Of course." Monica laughed, wrapping Annie in a big hug. "God helps those who use their talents well. You trusted His love and God came through . . ."

". . . as He always does," finished Tess.

A breath of wind blew through the open window, stirring the pages of the dictionary. One by one, they lifted and turned—to the page with the most important word of all. F, A, I, T, H, 'faith'—meaning "belief and trust in God."

Then, another ruffle of wind—and rustle of wings—and a snow-white dove soared out the window into the twilight sky.